D1264129

BIKER CITY

BY ANTHONY MASTERS

ILLUSTRATED BY HARRIET BUCKLEY

Librarian Reviewer
Kathleen Baxter
Children's Literature Consultant,
formerly with Anoka County Library, MN
BA College of Saint Catherine, St. Paul, MN
MA in Library Science, University of Minnesota

Reading Consultant
Elizabeth Stedem
Educator/Consultant, Colorado Springs, CO
MA in Elementary Education, University of Denver, CO

STONE ARCH BOOKS
MINNEAPOLIS SAN DIEGO

First published in the United States in 2007
by Stone Arch Books,
151 Good Counsel Drive, P.O. Box 669,
Mankato, Minnesota 56002.
www.stonearchbooks.com

Published by arrangement with
Barrington Stoke Ltd, Edinburgh.

Library of Congress Cataloging-in-Publication Data
Masters, Anthony, 1940–
[Tod in Biker City]
Biker City / by Anthony Masters; illustrated by Harriet Buckley.
p. cm. — (Pathway Books)
Originally published under title: Tod in Biker City.
Summary: When his father disappears from their desert wasteland home where water is scarce, Todd must search for him while braving the elements and evading gangs of outlaw bikers.
ISBN-13: 978-1-59889-108-9 (hardcover)
ISBN-10: 1-59889-108-1 (hardcover)
ISBN-13: 978-1-59889-252-9 (paperback)
ISBN-10: 1-59889-252-5 (paperback)
[1. Science fiction.] I. Buckley, Harriet, 1974–, ill. II. Title. III. Series.
PZ7.M423875Bi 2006
[Fic]—dc22 2006004778

Art Director: Heather Kindseth
Cover Graphic Designer and Illustrator: Brann Garvey
Interior Graphic Designer: Kay Fraser

1 2 3 4 5 6 11 10 09 08 07 06

Printed in the United States of America.

TABLE OF CONTENTS

CHAPTER 1

WAITING FOR DAD

"When will Dad get back?" asked Todd, nervously.

"I'm sure he'll be here soon," his mom told him.

Todd gazed out the window and down to the beach with its piles of rotting weeds and white fish bones. There was no life there because it hadn't rained for a very long time. The sea was far away now.

It gets harder every day to find water.
Are we all going to die?

"Todd, Dad won't come back just because you want him to," his mom went on.

Todd Hunter was 13. His dad had a gift that others did not have. He could find water under the ground. He had a special stick that he held in his hands. It moved by itself when water was near.

There was very little water anywhere, and many people had died from thirst already. There was panic. People would do anything to get water. It was not safe to live in the cities, so Todd and his family went to live by the sea.

Todd lived with his mom and dad in a house near the beach.

Years ago, lots of people used to visit. Now, no one came.

There were miles of sand. Near the road, the trees were black and dead. There was no green to be seen because there was no fresh water.

"I'm scared that the Bikers may have gotten Dad," said Todd. "They've been looking for someone to find water for them."

"Don't worry too much about it. Your dad can look after himself," said his mom.

But Todd knew she was scared, too.

"I'm going to take the beach buggy and go look for him," said Todd.

He needed a drink of water badly.

It was always like this. He and his mom had to share what little water they had.

Todd drove his beach buggy over the sand hills to the road. Then he heard the sound of an engine. It wasn't Dad's jeep. It was a bike.

Todd came to a stop behind a rock, just as a Biker came around the corner. The bike was large, black, and shiny.

The Biker was dressed in black, and he had a gang symbol painted on his dark helmet.

The Biker stopped and reached in his bag for a bottle of water. He took a long drink.

Todd watched him stretch out his arms and yawn.

The Biker turned his bike around and drove back the way he had come.

I hope he doesn't find Dad, thought Todd.

The Bikers were outside the law. They traveled in gangs. They robbed people and beat them up to get their water.

Todd waited until he could no longer hear the sound of the engine. Then he drove home in his beach buggy. As he drove back, Todd looked up at the gray sky. He gave a shiver in spite of the heat.

Thank God, Todd got home safely.

CHAPTER 2

SCORCHER

"I think that horrible, hot, dry wind is coming back," said Mom, when Todd got home. "We may have to go down to the basement and take some food with us."

Todd hated that wind. It was so hot that it was called a *scorcher*.

"And Dad's still not back," Todd said sadly. It was awful for Dad to be out when the *scorcher* swept in from the sea.

"I guess something's kept him," said his mom.

Todd decided not to tell her that he'd seen a Biker. It would just make her more scared.

Todd did not sleep much that night. Did the bikers get his dad? Was his dad being forced to find water for them?

When Todd did sleep, he could hear his dad in his dreams. "Help me, Todd! You've got to help me," he was saying. In his dreams, Todd tried to run to his dad, but his feet sank into the sand.

When he finally woke up, Todd ran into his parents' room.

Dad was not there.

"Where is he?" asked Todd.

"Not home yet," Mom replied. She was looking out the window. "But the *scorcher* is coming now."

Todd gazed at the steel gray sky. These winds were so hot and dry that they could burn away human flesh.

"I've put all we need in the basement," said his mom. "Let's get down there. Dad will be okay."

Todd and his mom sat in the basement and looked at the sand spilling through the wall. "I'm sure he found somewhere to get shelter from the wind," Mom went on.

If the Bikers haven't gotten him, thought Todd to himself. But out loud, he said to his mom, "He'll be home soon."

The sound of the wind had grown so loud that they could hardly hear themselves speak. It was very hot in the basement. Mom told Todd to drink some water from the jar on the floor.

"Here, Mom," said Todd. "You have some water, too." But she shook her head.

Hours later, the wind blew itself out and was silent.

They went upstairs. The house was okay. Through the window, they could see piles of sand against the front door. Then Todd heard a roar.

"That can't be the wind coming back," began Mom.

Todd knew what it was. He could see the Bikers riding toward their house across the sand hills.

CHAPTER 3

UNWANTED VISITORS

"Quick, go out the back door, Mom. The Bikers are on their way. We can hide in the woods!" yelled Todd.

"Why are they coming here?" asked his mom.

"To see if they can find any maps or papers to show them where there's still water," replied Todd.

"Dad keeps them in the safe," said Mom.

I have to look after Todd.
But I don't know what to do.
I have to look after Mom, but I'm really scared.

"They could blow it open," Todd told her.

They looked at each other.

"The Bikers must have gotten Dad," said Mom. "Otherwise, why are they coming here?"

"We don't have time to talk. Let's go," Todd replied.

Todd and his mom ran outside and hid in a grove of bare, black trees.

They ducked down as they heard the Bikers coming closer to the house. Then the Bikers stopped and switched off their engines. There was no sound for a long time.

"What's going on?" asked Mom.

"I can't see," said Todd.

Then they heard the sound of a door being kicked in. They waited for ages. Something was being dragged out of the house. There was a soft thump.

"That's the safe," said Todd in a quiet voice.

There was another long silence. Then they heard a loud bang.

"That was the safe," he said. "They blew it open."

Did the Bikers hurt Dad? Did they try to make him talk? Did they come to the house because he wouldn't tell them anything?

The engines revved up again.

"One of them may have stayed behind as a lookout," said Todd.

"I'm going to sneak over to the house," he added. "You stay here. We don't want them to get both of us."

Todd went slowly up to the house in case there was still anyone there. The door had been broken in, and the safe lay open on the sand.

Todd was angry. What right did the Bikers have to break into his home like this? And what did they do to his dad?

"I told you to wait in the woods," he said to his mom as she came up to the house.

"Don't you tell me what to do." She was very upset. "Just look at this mess. I'm fed up with it! We have to go and find your father."

"We?" Todd asked.

"Yes. You go north, and I'll go south," his mom told him. "He could be anywhere."

"Biker City?" asked Todd.

"Could be," she said.

"I'll find it if I go south," Todd told her. "Good thing I've got the buggy. That's faster than your old car."

"Please be careful," she begged.

"We've got to find him, Mom," said Todd.

"What can we do against the Bikers? It's hopeless," replied Mom.

Will Mom
be okay on
her own?

CHAPTER 4

ALONE

When they reached the main road, they stopped to say goodbye. They had filled their bags with as much food and water as they could carry.

"Don't take any big risks," his mom told him.

"It's all a risk now, Mom," Todd said. "You know that."

She began to cry.

Then Todd's mom got into her old car. "I know," she said. "Please be careful, Toddy."

Todd's mom hadn't called him that in years. Not since their old home had been burned down by the hot wind, and they'd had to find somewhere else to live.

Mom took off to the north. She waved until she was out of sight.

Todd revved up his buggy and sped off over the sand hills.

Soon he saw a dark shape. As he got closer, Todd saw that it was a water tower. The Bikers' symbol was painted in red on the side.

Todd knew it would be crazy to drive any closer. He would have to hide the buggy in the sand hills and walk.

Dad must be somewhere down there.
Please let him be okay.

In front of him, the sun was blazing down on a heap of rusty old cars, buses, and trucks.

Todd hid behind a pile of rocks. Where did the Bikers go? He thought he heard something move behind him. A few yards away, there was a pile of old oil drums. Did the noise come from there?

He couldn't see anything because the sun was too bright. He turned back and gazed at the scrap yard where the Bikers lived. Where were they?

Most important of all, what did they do with Dad?

Then something large and solid hit Todd from behind. It pushed him down into the hot sand. Todd rolled over.

The stranger attacking him fell over on his back. Todd jumped to his feet and threw himself on top of the boy, who was dressed in the black gear of the Bikers.

Todd landed with his knees on the boy's chest and held down his arms. The boy tried to shake him off, but Todd was too strong for him.

"Where are the Bikers?" Todd asked.

"I don't know," the boy answered.

Todd pressed down, and the boy howled with pain.

"Where are they?" Todd demanded.

"I don't know," said the boy again.

"You've got to tell me," said Todd.

The boy shook his head. "I won't."

He's one of them.
He must know where they are.

Todd had a quick thought. The boy looked scared. Did he think Todd was going to really hurt him?

"Do you want some water?" Todd asked.

"You got some?" The boy's lips were dry.

"Two bottles," Todd told him.

"That much?" said the boy.

"What's your name?" asked Todd.

"Billy." He looked up, and Todd could tell Billy didn't trust him. "How do I know you've got water?"

"Keep still, and I'll show you," said Todd.

Todd reached over and pulled a bottle of water out of his bag.

"I'll trade you for this," said Todd.

"What for?" asked Billy.

"You have to tell me where they've taken my dad," said Todd.

Billy looked at the water. He licked his dry lips. He was longing for a drink.

"Give me the water first," he said.

"No way." Todd shook the bottle, and the water sloshed around inside. "Not until you tell me where they took my dad and how to get there."

Billy gave in. "They're down at the old tin mine. It's on the other side of the city. They found your dad there looking for water."

"He thought he was safe because we were away on a raid," Billy added.

"Why are you out here alone?" asked Todd.

"I stole some water from the tower. Not much. Just a few drops, but they were mad at me, so they chased me away," said Billy.

"So, how do I find the tin mine?" Todd asked.

"You go right through Biker City," Billy replied. "There's a sign for the old tin mine. Now, where's that water?"

Todd gave him the bottle. Billy drank as if he would never stop. "That's all you get," said Todd.

But Billy kept on drinking.

Todd grabbed the bottle and told Billy to save some for later.

"One thing," Billy said.

"What's that?" asked Todd.

"Don't let them know I told you," said Billy. "They'll kill me."

Todd went back to the buggy and drove off through Biker City. He looked back at Billy. The boy looked so lonely that Todd felt sorry for him.

Todd had to leave and find the old tin mine. He had to find Dad.

MAP
CITY
OF BIKER
THE HILLS
OLD TIN
MINE
TIN MINE
BIKER CITY
to the
dunes

CHAPTER 5

A Cry in the Dark

A hot wind blew the sand into Todd's eyes. They began to sting badly. Then at the very edge of Biker City, he saw a sign that read **Tin Mine**.

Todd drove on. He came to a pile of old cars, which gave him some cover from the sun. It was very, very hot. Todd was scared that the Bikers might come back at any moment.

Todd looked ahead. There was silence everywhere. Just a few seagulls were flying over the bare fields.

Slowly he drove on. Then he saw the shabby, old tin mine. There were lots of motorcycles parked there, so Todd drove the buggy back the way he had come.

When he got back to the pile of smashed cars, he hid the buggy behind them. Then Todd jumped out onto the sand and ran back to the mine again. He checked to see if the beach buggy could be seen. Yes, part of the buggy stuck out from behind the cars, but there was no time to fix it.

The Bikers were coming out of the mine. Todd hid himself in a ditch behind a pile of sand.

Todd was scared that the Bikers would see the buggy sticking out of the pile of cars. If they did see it, they would come and look for him.

Todd laid flat in the ditch as the Bikers raced past him. The dust from their motorcycles choked him. When he lifted his head, Todd saw them riding away, bent low over their bikes.

The Bikers had been going too fast to see the buggy.

Phew, that was close, Todd said to himself. Too close!

Todd got to his feet. He went back behind the pile of cars and hid the buggy better. Then Todd began to walk slowly back to the tin mine.

He looked out for danger with every step.

When he got to the mine, there seemed to be no one around. But the silence scared him. His heart thumped.

Todd walked to an open mine shaft and looked down into the dark hole. What was he going to do now?

Todd laid down and stuck his head into the black shaft. He knew the Bikers might creep up on him at any moment.

Earlier, he hadn't seen Billy coming, but he had been able to deal with him.

Of course, he was much stronger than Billy. Todd knew he would be no match against a real Biker.

"Dad?" he yelled. "Are you down there? Can you hear me, Dad?"

Silence. Maybe his dad wasn't down there after all.

Todd tried again. "Dad," he shouted. "Can you hear me?"

Then he heard a reply from far down below.

Todd yelled down the shaft again. This time he was sure he heard his dad's voice.

"Dad! Hang on. I'm coming down!" yelled Todd.

He could still hear his dad shouting down in the shaft, but he couldn't understand what he was saying.

Todd didn't wait any longer. He stood up and grabbed the top of the ladder. Down he went, into the dark.

I've got to help
Dad get out
of here!

CHAPTER 6

DESCENT INTO DARKNESS

Todd began to feel more and more safe as he climbed down. He was going faster and faster when he came to a sudden stop. He had reached the end of the ladder. There was just a black hole below him.

If only Todd had a flashlight with him. It was dark all around him, and there was only a little light from the top of the shaft.

Todd looked down and felt scared. Then a dim light shined up at him. He had found Dad at last.

"They've chopped off the bottom of the ladder, so I can't get out," Dad shouted.

"I'll jump!" Todd called down.

"No, go back! Please, Todd," said Dad. "There's no way you can help me."

"You know I'd never leave you down here," said Todd.

"You'll only get trapped yourself. Go back home. I'll figure something out," said Dad.

"I'm coming down, Dad. I'm going to jump," Todd said.

"Wait!" Dad told him. "Let me move over so I can catch you."

Todd looked down. What if he broke a leg? They'd both be trapped down there. Still, what could he do? He had to jump.

"Are you ready?" asked Dad.

"I'm coming. Now," said Todd as he let go of the ladder. The fall seemed to take a long time. Then he felt a thump as he landed on Dad. They both fell to the ground.

Todd was lying on top of his dad, and Dad had his arms around him, hugging him. Todd got to his feet. He was okay. Nothing was broken. He picked up his dad's flashlight and shined it on Dad, who was finding it hard to stand up.

"Dad, are you okay?" Todd asked in a panic.

"Yes, you just knocked the wind out of me," Dad said. He was panting.

Todd sighed in relief. "How did you get here?" he asked.

"I was looking for water, and the Bikers found me. They said I had to work for them, but I said no," Dad told him.

Todd could see that his dad's face had marks all over it.

"They beat you up!" Todd cried.

"I wasn't going to give in," said Dad. "I said I wouldn't work for them. They cut off the bottom part of the ladder so that I couldn't get out."

"They're gone now, but they said they'd come back tomorrow as soon as it was light," added Dad.

“What are they going to do then?” asked Todd. He was scared.

“They said I should think things over. If I won’t find water for them, they’ll kill me.”

“Have you found any yet?” Todd asked.

“Come with me. I have something to show you,” said Dad.

There's water somewhere.
But how much, and can we get at it?

CHAPTER 7

DANGEROUS DISCOVERY

There wasn't much light coming from Dad's flashlight now. Dad set off down a tunnel, and Todd went after him. Then Dad stopped and picked up the stick that he used to find water. When he pointed it at the wall, the stick began to twist and turn.

"That means there's water on the other side," said Dad.

"How do we get at it?" asked Todd.

"I've got two hammers with me," said Dad. "The rock's already cracked here. If we work hard enough, we might be able to smash a hole through to the other side."

"Now aren't you glad I found you?" said Todd.

"Yes," said Dad, "but your mom will be very upset by now. She won't know where you are."

"She'll still be out looking for you," Todd told him.

Todd could see tears in his dad's eyes. "Let's get to work, then," said Dad.

They hammered away at the rock for over an hour. "I can smell water," Dad said.

Todd could only smell the stale air of the tunnel. The hole they had made in the rock seemed very small. Todd felt worn out.

They began to hammer away again. Dad's flashlight had gone out a long time ago. Luckily, Todd's watch lit up in the dark. "It's the middle of the night. How much longer are we going to keep going?" asked Todd.

"We've got to work faster. The Bikers will be back as soon as the sun's up," Dad told him.

We now have some hope, but we're not safe yet.
Good old Dad, I knew he'd get us out.

CHAPTER 8

SWIM FOR YOUR LIFE!

After two more hours of hard work, a large chunk of rock fell away. There was a splash as it landed on the other side.

"We made it!" said Dad. "The hole is big enough that we can wiggle through it."

He was right.

Todd felt much better.

As Dad began to slip through the hole in the rock, they both heard a noise far back in the mine shaft.

"You said they wouldn't come until it got light, Dad," whispered Todd.

"They must need water badly," Dad replied, as Todd climbed through the hole behind him.

The water came up to their knees in the dark space behind the rock wall. They felt their way along a winding tunnel, wading through the water. Then a beam of light cut into the dark.

"There's water in there!" yelled a Biker.

"Go back and find somebody small enough to go through this hole," Todd heard one of them say.

"Keep going," Dad told Todd, as they worked their way along the edge of the tunnel. "We've got to go where the water goes."

The water was getting deep. It was up to their waists. Then Todd hit his head on something.

"This must be the end of the tunnel," he said.

"No, the tunnel hasn't ended," Dad told him. "It's just that the water goes under the ground here."

"This is the end of us," said Todd in a quiet voice.

"The water may come out into a cave." Dad was more hopeful.

"Then let's dive," said Todd. "The Bikers don't need you now. They'll get us both if we go back."

Todd bent down to feel the thin gap between the water and the rock.

How long could they swim under the water and stay alive with no air?

"I'll go first," said Todd, and he took a deep breath.

Once he was under the water, Todd was thrown from one side of the tunnel to the other. He hit the rocky sides again and again. He could not breathe. How far did they have to swim before they came out into the air again?

CHAPTER 9

WHERE TO NOW?

Todd was sure he was going to drown. He felt his lungs were about to burst. Mom's going to be left alone, he thought. She would never see him or Dad again.

Then, just as Todd couldn't hold out any longer, he was pushed out of the tunnel and into the air. He could breathe again. His father bumped into him as he, too, came out of the tunnel.

They were standing in water up to their waists in a huge cave. A pale light glowed in the distance.

"It's like magic," said Dad.

They pulled themselves out of the water and onto a rock ledge. They laid down on their backs and filled their lungs with fresh air. By the pale light, they could see that their clothes were ripped, and their bodies were skinned and bruised. They had been badly knocked around.

"Where are we?" asked Todd.

"This must be the Hollow Hill," Dad told him.

"I thought it was just a kid's story that it was hollow," said Todd.

"Now we know it's true," Dad said.

They turned over and drank from the water until they were full.

"Too bad the Bikers followed us and found the water," said Todd.

"They'll try to take it all for themselves. It won't be safe around here any longer. We have to find somewhere else to live," said Dad.

Then the sound of a motor reached their ears. They hid behind a rock. Of course, the Bikers must know the story of the Hollow Hill, too, thought Todd.

"Let's get back into the water," he said and was about to move when Dad grabbed him.

"Wait, that's not a motorcycle. It sounds more like your beach buggy," Dad said.

He was right. The buggy was bumping over the rocky floor of the cave. It stopped at the water's edge. But who was driving it?

It was Billy, and Todd's mom was sitting beside him.

"What do you think you're doing, Billy? You steal my buggy, and you kidnap my mom," yelled Todd.

"No, that's not it at all," Mom called as Todd and Dad worked their way toward her.

"Billy told me he knew where you were, but he was scared to go near the mine shaft because of the Bikers. Then he found the entrance to this cave. But how did you get here, and why are your clothes torn?" asked Mom.

"It's a long story," Todd told her.

"Let me get at that water," said Billy, and he ran over and drank and drank.

Todd, Mom, and Dad were smiling and hugging each other.

Then Billy looked up. "The Bikers are going to kill me for this," he said.

Dad said slowly, "So why don't you come with us? We have to find a new place to live."

"That would be great," said Mom. She looked over at Dad, and he nodded.

"If that's okay with you, Todd," Dad asked him.

"It's okay with me," Todd said.

He was sure he could see tears in Billy's eyes.

About the Author

Anthony Masters wrote many novels, short stories, and nonfiction books for children and young adults. His most recent works included a children's version of Shakespeare's play *Hamlet* and a young adult series on World War II. Anthony Masters died in 2003.

About the Illustrator

Harriet Buckley is a very busy artist. After earning a master's degree in illustration at the Edinburgh College of Art in Scotland, she has worked non-stop illustrating books, magazines, and comics. Harriet likes creating artwork digitally on computers, and has also animated numerous commercials and short films. She has even painted an "optical-illusion"-style mural for a private home in Holland.

Glossary

blazing (BLAYZ-ing)—very hot

descent (di-SENT)—a journey down

grove (GROHV)—a group of trees growing near each other

hollow (HOL-oh)—having an empty space inside

ledge (LEJ)—a narrow, flat shelf

lookout (LUK-out)—someone who keeps watch over something

raid (RAYD)—a sudden attack to search for and take something

revved (REVD)—gave more fuel to an engine to make it run fast and loud

safe (SAYF)—a strong box for locking up valuable items

symbol (SIM-buhl)—a design or mark that stands for something

Discussion Questions

1. In the beginning of the book, we learn that it hasn't rained for a very long time. What year do you think it might be? What might have happened to make the rains stop and the Earth become so dry?

2. The Bikers come to Todd's house to blow open Dad's safe. What do you think they find inside?

3. Billy tells Todd where to find his father in exchange for a bottle of water. Do you think Billy just wants the water, or could there be other reasons he helps Todd?

Writing Prompts

1. Maybe Todd should have left a note, in case Dad gets home while he and Mom are out looking for him. Pretend you are Todd, and write a note for Dad telling him what happened and why you and Mom left home.

2. Think of a time when you were really thirsty. Write about why you were so thirsty, and how it felt and tasted when you finally got a cool drink of water.

3. Billy and Mom arrive in the cave on Todd's beach buggy. Write a paragraph about what happened when Mom first met Billy.

Internet Sites

Do you want to know more about subjects related to this book? Or are you interested in learning about other topics? Then check out FactHound, a fun, easy way to find Internet sites.

Our investigative staff has already sniffed out great sites for you!

Here's how to use FactHound:

1. Visit *www.facthound.com*
2. Select your grade level.
3. To learn more about subjects related to this book, type in the book's ISBN number: **1598891081**.
4. Click the **Fetch It** button.

FactHound will fetch the best Internet sites for you!